THEFT

I thought again about the police. They were pretty clever, and Mam's biggest nightmare was that we would get into trouble. The boys were looking at me and slyly fingering the coins, dropping them from one hand to the other.

'Look,' I said desperately, 'you can take the books back, every one, if you like. I tell you what, I'll even take the books back myself, if only you'll take them coins back.'

'Alright,' Porky said cockily.
I shuddered at the thought of those dark back alleys behind the high street.
'Yes,' I said, cool as I could.

Wendy Robertson

Theft

CAROUSEL EDITOR: ANNE WOOD

TRANSWORLD PUBLISHERS LTD
A NATIONAL GENERAL COMPANY

THEFT

A CAROUSEL BOOK 0 552 52025 x

First publication in Great Britain

PRINTING HISTORY

Carousel edition published 1972

Copyright © Wendy Robertson 1972
Illustrations © Transworld Publishers Ltd 1972

This book is set in Baskerville 12/14 pt.

Carousel Books are published by Transworld Publishers Ltd.,
Cavendish House, 57–59 Uxbridge Road, Ealing, London W.5

Made and printed in Great Britain by
Richard Clay (The Chaucer Press), Ltd., Bungay, Suffolk.

**NOTE: The Australian price appearing on the
back cover is the recommended retail price**

THEFT

Robert found a seat on the old bus, and looked out of the window at the gaunt height of the building he had just left. This new school was different from the old one, just like everything else. He settled down and the bus began its swaying journey. He watched the conductor, tall and thin cheeked, with a hat too big for him, make his way down the bus.

'Sixpence-to-Green-End,' he mumbled, and ran the words together on purpose.

'Yes, sir.' The conductor nearly bowed as he handed him his ticket, and grinned as he counted out the change. Robert knew that he, like the rest, was laughing at his accent.

It had happened at school as well. They had laughed behind their hands, called him fancypants to his face. They had echoed his words, saying in awed whispers, 'What dja' think he means, hinny?'

Until he had come North with his mother, Robert had not thought much about the way

7

people talked. It was rotten feeling like a foreigner here, although he was still in England. He had cried the first night in bed. When his mother came to sit beside his bed, as usual, she asked what was the matter. He shouted back at her.

'Why did we have to come up here anyway? We were alright where we were.'

'I suppose we were, but your Dad did want you to grow up here. Seemed to think you'd take to it. And the people.'

'Well I don't like it. The people are funny and the places are nasty.' He was choking now.

'I'm sure you'll get used to it. Just remember your Dad grew up here, and he's turned out O.K. hasn't he?'

Robert rubbed his face on the sheet. His Dad was great really. He was a doctor working in South America just then. He would not be back for another three months. He had talked to him about being the man about the house, before he went.

Mother tucked him in briskly, without really looking at him. 'That's better. We can't have big boys of nine crying for nothing can we?'

Then, Robert knew she was upset too. She didn't usually talk in that soft way.

*   *   *

'Yours next stop, son.' The conductor shouted down the gangway. He looked out of the window.

It was dark but you could see the pavements, in the shine of the streetlamps, and people more like shadows darting by. The old bus sighed to a stop as he walked along the gangway, clutching his schoolbag. Even that was a new one, and had made the boys at school laugh even more.

He could see his aunt waiting at the bus stop, very tall with wild black hair, and a red sort of smock. He had met her once before, at the new flat. She had come on the day they arrived and helped to sort the furniture, and filled the place with talk and laughing. Mother had smiled when she'd gone.

'Noisy but nice,' she'd said.

Now, Auntie May folded him in a big hug, like being wrapped in a rug.

'Robert! I'm so pleased you have come. I thought you'd miss the bus, or get the wrong one, or be late out of school . . .'

'Mammy, he's not an idiot.' The owner of the cross voice was a tall girl with fierce red hair, standing just behind Auntie May. The two other girls were there as well.

'I'm so sorry, Robert! This is Betty, who's twelve and very bossy, and Gabbi who is eleven and quite bossy, and Pearl who is nine, like you, and not bossy at all.' They were all so big, even Pearl. The two eldest both had that dark marmalade hair, just like his, but with thick fringes down on to their eyes, and Pearl was like a small version of her mother with black hair sticking out all over the place, and long stalky legs.

It was Pearl who put her hand on his arm. 'Come on. We've been waiting ages, and its pikelets for tea, all dripping with butter.'

'Pikelets?' That was the first word he had managed to get in since he got off the bus.

Auntie May laughed. 'You call them crumpets where you come from. I can see we'll have to educate you, my lad.' That was the first time in a week he didn't feel bad about being different.

*   *   *

They had the pikelets, and some cream cakes, followed by apples and cream, and all the time the girls talked and talked. They asked Robert about school, then told him about theirs. Auntie May asked him about his mother, and laughed when he said the shopkeepers couldn't understand her. All the girls made such a noise, but it was that kind of a buzz that made him want to laugh and laugh.

After tea, they all sat round the fire and suddenly Betty stood up.

'I forgot, Mammy. Sorting out that suitcase that was under my bed. For dressing up things, you know. Anyway, I found the funniest thing.'

'What was that, then?'

Betty was at the door. 'I'll get it.'

Two minutes later she was back again. She threw what looked like a small leather bag on to her mother's knee. Robert crowded round with the girls. It hadn't taken long to discover that it was no good being shy or holding back in this house.

Auntie May picked the bag up thoughtfully. It was soft, more like leather than cloth. She opened the drawstring top, and tumbled a yellow coin into her lap. Robert's hand was first there. The coin was very heavy. It had the head of a strange king, a history-book king, but still, it looked like a brand new coin. The words, and the outline of the head, were clear and sharp. He ran his thumb over the surface.

Pearl was the first to speak. 'Is it gold?'

'Oh, yes,' Auntie May sounded quiet, almost dreamy. 'I should imagine it's very valuable, as it's in mint condition. Coincidence, it turning up to-day. I thought we had lost it in the last move.'

'Why a coincidence?' demanded Gabbi.

'You'll see.' She looked round at all of them, and looking especially hard at Robert as she said, 'Would you like to hear how I got that coin? It's rather a long story.'

Everybody shouted 'Yes', and they all sat down, the three girls on the floor, and Robert on the arm of Auntie May's chair. He felt very easy and comfortable, as though he'd been there a hundred times before.

She looked at him and smiled. 'To tell you this story, I'll have to take you right out of this house.' He looked for the first time at the room which was

very comfortable and cluttered, and thought that the house must be quite large if you could judge by the hall, and the length of this room. 'I'll have to take you over to the other end of the town, to a spot that's all cleared now for a car park. When I was ten, Robert, I lived in a house there. It was a narrow street with a pub at the end. The houses were small, maybe primitive, and I lived in one of them with my brother and my mother.' Her eyes were bright and she didn't seem to be seeing them any more. She was rubbing the coin between two fingers.

*　　*　　*

Auntie May talked quietly, but the children sat in silence. 'Compared with this place I suppose that that house was tiny—a small living room and a built-on kitchen, and one big bedroom divided into two by a wood partition. But we never thought it was small. We lived there quite content, my mam and our Teddy and me. Mam was out best part of the day at her job at the factory, and most nights she helped along at the pub.

But Teddy and I had some wonderful times.

At the time of the gold coin, I would be about ten, and Teddy was eleven—big for his age with that awful ginger hair. I suppose he was pretty good, for a brother, because he took me all over with him.

We used to go down to the wood most days when we weren't at school, and have the most marvellous adventures. That wood's a little copse beside those new houses, now, with the dirty old stream running through it. The wood seemed much bigger then, and the stream was much wider.

Teddy liked to go from one end of the wood to the other without touching the path. We could only step where no one had ever stepped before. Sometimes we would do this, by threading through the trees high on the slopes, sometimes by walking without our shoes through the stream. It was always icy cold. The stones in the bottom were sharp and often cut our feet.

Teddy knew all the places where the small animals lived. They were mostly rabbits or voles, or an occasional hedgehog. Once we saw the black and white flash of a badger sliding under a hedge. Teddy was so excited that he left nailmarks in my arms, where he had grabbed me to make me stand still.

We had a den in the wood, made from two remaining walls of a broken down old hut. Teddy had sawed branches to replace the demolished walls, and we had begged a tarpaulin from Kelly, the old cartman, and dragged it up to the den to cover the branches.

It was cosy inside, as long as it didn't rain too hard. If we stayed late, Teddy would light a fire, to get us warmed through before we set off for home. I used to cough and cough with the smoke, but Teddy took no notice, and never coughed himself.

In the summer holidays we sometimes went up there for the whole day, with sandwiches and bottles of water. Once Teddy spent nearly a week skinning a dead fox we had found under a hedge. The smell of the skin got worse and worse and in the end I refused to go inside the den, the smell was so bad. It was months before that smell really faded.

Apart from the animals, our favourite thing in the wood was looking for treasure. Teddy would decide on a likely spot, write directions, and draw a map. Then we would follow the instructions and dig in the latest suitable spot. I did most of the digging, with a shovel we kept in the den. It had been a garden spade, but the handle had broken. Teddy had bound it with string and it made a very useful shovel. We never did find any treasure but Teddy was always hopeful. You never know what went on on this spot a hundred, or two hundred years ago, he would say.

One day in October—potato picking holiday, it was—we were making our way down to the edge of the town which led to the wood. The air was very cold, and our breath danced on the air as we talked. The sun was struggling to shine, but only managed to settle a cold white glow over the narrow houses and the greyish pavements. Teddy was hurrying along to keep warm, and I was breathlessly trying to keep up, as usual.

'Hey, Ted!' There were heavy footsteps behind, and a large shape hurtled past me. Teddy turned round and a grin split his face.

'Now, Porky!'

'What you doing down this end, Ted?'

'We're just going for a look down the wood.'

'We?' The boy called Porky turned to look at me, as though I had just appeared out of the air, like a winter genie. I saw his face and I didn't like him. It was fat, and he had one of those awful haircuts they had then, that made them look like prisoners.

'Me sister.' Teddy waved a hand at me as though I were just part of the pavement, and went on talking to Porky. 'Where are you off, then?'

'No-where. Just wandering about.'

They were quiet for a minute and I held my breath. Then Teddy spoke. 'You like to have a look down the wood with us?'

'Hey, yes.' So the two of them just fell into step and I was still walking behind.

When we got to the edge of the wood, Teddy led the way down to the path, and I realised that we weren't going our usual secret way. This gave me hope. Surely Teddy wouldn't take this boy to the den.

We were walking in thick leaves. Only the lower branches and the shrubs seemed to have hung on to

their summer clothes. The high branches coming over our heads like interlacing fingers, were bare and black against the whitish sky.

The two boys leapt and shouted and yodelled as they walked along. They hung from thick branches and dodged around trees. They shouted and wrestled with each other, and dawdled so much that I was soon well ahead of them. I was mad. Teddy had never let me make any noise in the wood, as it would scare away the animals, so that he would miss seeing them.

'May! May!' Teddy was shouting, waving his arm to tell me to go back. I went back very slowly. I had purposely passed the turn off to the den, in the hope that Teddy would not go there, not when this boy was with him.

'Where are you going?'

'Up the den. Porky wants to see the den.' Teddy was already running to catch up with his friend. When I reached the den, they were already settled in. Porky was sitting on one of the old logs we used for stools, and Teddy was busy at the brick hearth we had made, building a fire from dry leaves and small sticks.

'Hey, this is great!' Porky was turning over the fox skin, stiff and awful by now it was. He looked around the dark den, only lit by the strip of light where we had dragged back the tarpaulin to get in.

'Do you ever cook anything on your fire?' he

demanded.

'We haven't yet.' Teddy blew at the little flame.

'Well, we could bring some taties and roast them, maybe even some soup ...'

'Good idea.' Teddy laughed, and I was furious again. I had asked and asked him about cooking on the fire, and he never would, saying that that was girl-stuff.

After that I just never spoke. All the time they were playing and leaping around like a pair of red indians, I just collected some twigs, and made a few piles of stones, and sat around generally.

I could have leapt with joy when Teddy finally said we should be getting back. Porky didn't want to go.

'I'm just beginning to enjoy myself,' he moaned.

'We can come another day. Tomorrow?'

'Why not?'

Porky walked all the way home with Teddy, and they dawdled so much, that I had been in the house a good five minutes when Teddy came in. I had lit the gasfire, put the kettle on, and was laying the table when he finally shot through the thick curtain that separated the little lobby from the living room.

He threw himself on to the couch that stood facing the fire.

'Hey. What a great afternoon!'

I put the bread and a dish of margarine in the middle of the table.

'Who was that lad, anyway?' I tried not to sound very interested.

'Porky? He used to be in the next class above, at school, before he went up to the big school. Must be more than twelve I should think.'

'There's nothing special about being twelve.'

'Maybe not. But Porky's alright, isn't he?'

I opened my mouth to answer, when my mam pushed her way through the curtain, and swept in, in her old red coat with its fur collar. She had the same old packet of fish and chips in her hand, the same old grin on her face.

'Alright kids? Had a good day? Thank goodness you've got the kettle on. I'm just parched for a cup of tea. Been rushed off my feet all day . . .'

She talked on and on, and I settled down to enjoy my fish and chips. As usual, the house seemed warmer and much more cheerful when she was there, and for a while I even forgot about the fat boy called Porky who had spoiled my afternoon.

* * *

Porky spoiled my afternoon and he spoiled my evening too. Mam had done herself up a bit, and gone along to the pub. The room was warming up nicely, and the wireless was on quite loud. Teddy and I were playing Monopoly. It was a tatty old game that had been second-hand when Mam had got it for Teddy when he was eight.

We played most nights, and Teddy usually won. He often made up rules, as soon as I had broken them, and kept telling me to use my brain, use my brain. This night, I was just about to get the better of Teddy for once when there was a big knock on the door. We looked at each other. No one ever called at night. Queer thing. At last Teddy got up to open it.

As soon as I heard Porky's voice, I started to put the paper money back into the box. He did not come in, but by sitting well back on the settee, I could hear quite well.

'You coming out, then?' he was saying.

'Out where?' There wasn't much to do in Benfield in the evening in those days.

'Just out.' Porky sounded a bit narky. 'There's plenty to do if you look. 'Nt you ever been out at night then?'

'Course I have.' Teddy put on a cocky voice. 'Just that there's not much going, that's all. Hang on, I'll get me coat.'

He flashed into the room and grabbed it from its usual peg. 'Just off out, kid. I'll give you a game tomorrow night maybe.'

'But Teddy,' I wailed, and I gulped to stop myself crying. He hated girls who cried, and we had had many a laugh at such softies.

'Don't bubble,' he said, scowling. I'll be back later. And just you dare tell Mam, about me going out!'

The front latch clicked and I was on my own. I jammed the Monopoly stuff back in the box and thought with hatred of that horrible Porky. He had spoiled everything that day, and it looked like he would spoil a few more things, before he had finished.

I lay down on the couch and cried and wailed and kicked and screamed. I kept bashing the back of the couch with my fist and just wishing it was Porky's fat face, not the lovely old brown leather. In the end I went off to sleep and dreamt that I was the captain of a boat, and Porky was sweeping water off the decks. The more he swept, the more water gushed back, and I laughed and laughed.

*   *   *

The door banged again, and I jumped up with a start, didn't know whether it was morning or night. My arms were cold, and I started to rub them. Teddy pushed his head round the curtain. 'Mam not in yet?'

'No. What time is it?'

'Townhall clock striking ten as I passed, so it must be nearly ten past. By, you look a mess.' He was in the room now, and I could see he was clutching a huge carrier bag.

'Yes. Been asleep for hours, and I'm not half cold. What's that?'

He threw the bag with a clunk on to the couch

beside me. 'They're for you. I know how much you like that sort of thing, so I brought them.'

I held the bag by its bottom, and tipped out the contents. There must have been twenty books there, all sizes. I looked up at Teddy, who was taking off his coat, and puffing and blowing with the cold.

'Well,' he said, 'I thought if ever you were in on your own, like tonight, you could maybe read them. I know how much you like books.'

I turned one of the books over. There was a picture on the hard cover of a little girl with long golden hair, dancing around in a blue floating sort of dress. The title was cut out in red above. *Tales of a Good Little Girl.* Inside, the printing looked very pretty but sort of old.

All the books were old in that same way. Funny little girls, in long clothes, and boys in things like jeans cut off at the knee. Some of the books were dampish, and going green at the edges, and they smelt a bit sickly. I clean forgot about Teddy as I turned the stiff pages, peered at the pictures, and made out the old-fashioned words.

There had never ever been this many books in the house at once. I had exactly six books, which lived upstairs on the table beside my bed. They were all the ones that Mam had bought me since I was about three. I had always loved and cared for them. I scrounged Sellotape to fix them when the backs began to go, and had finally backed them

with brown paper when they began to fall apart altogether. The two library books I borrowed every week were always on top of the pile, and, with their bright colours and new condition, made mine look shabby.

Teddy had often laughed at me and called me a book-miser. But I was a bit glad that he had thought of me when he found these queer old books. Found? I turned to Teddy.

'Where they from, Teddy? Where d'you get them?'

'Well . . .' We both heard our Mam's laugh from outside as she chatted to someone at our door. 'Hey. Get rid of them. Go put them upstairs or something.' He was piling the books back into the carrier as though they were poison.

*   *   *

Mam came in, the red coat still on, and her hair even wilder than usual. It must have been windy outside. 'By, it's windy!' She threw her coat over the back of a chair. 'You not got the kettle on, May? I do need that cup of tea tonight.'

I dashed into the kitchen and put the kettle on the jumpy gas flame. It was a very old kettle, with a thick rim of black round the bottom from years of boiling. The rim was first started when the water was boiled on a big black iron range we had had at first. According to Mam, the water from that kettle made a very special cup of tea. I messed around with the mugs and the teapot, and by the time I got back into the living room carrying the steaming mugs, Mam was settled in the best chair, with her feet up and her arms flopped over the chair arms like bits of rag.

It was the best time of day for me, and for Teddy I think too. No matter how tired she was, she always asked us what we'd been up to, and laughed at our stories. She told us all the terrible things that had happened at the factory or in the pub. Like the time George Mason had been tricked by his pals into balancing a pint of beer on his nose, with his hands tied behind his back. Then all his pals had walked out and left him.

Now Teddy was telling her about going down the woods. 'And we met this mate of mine. Porky. We had a great time.'

'Friend?' Mam frowned a bit at this. 'Now, Teddy, you be sure to take care of our May. Don't go running and leaving her! Do you hear?'

'Oh, Mam. I can't . . .'

'Yes, you can. You know there's no one to take care of her except you.'

Teddy groaned and sighed together, and I nearly shouted. 'I'm not a baby, you know.'

Mam smiled. 'I know you're not, love. But at least if you're with Teddy, I know where you are. Goodness knows I don't like going out to work. But just at the present time, I don't know how we would eat if I didn't.'

Both Teddy and I shut up at that. Things were hard and she never complained unless us two had a row. Then she always brought it up. It was a sure way to stop us tormenting each other. I sat back and lost myself in a favourite daydream of Mam being there on tap whenever I came home, or meeting me at the school-gate to take me to the shops, like many mothers I knew.

But our Mam would make up for it all on Sundays. We always did something special then, when we had her for every bit of the day. On fine days it would be a long walk, right away from the smoke of the town, into the country beyond, then beans on toast for tea. On wet days she would make up a special quiz which might have as many as fifty questions in it, and the winner could choose what to have for tea.

The best Sunday of all was once when we went on the bus to Durham to see the cathedral. The tall pillars like solid trees, reared up all about us, and the low chatter of the people around us sank into the thick walls and came out again as only the faintest whisper.

We climbed the hundreds of steps up the high cathedral tower. About forty steps from the top, Mam leaned against a window sill.

'Hey, kids, I've lost my puff. Can't get me breath at all. You go on, and I'll wait here.'

We raced on, up and up, and Teddy of course

was the first there. 'Look at this!' he kept shouting, 'Look at this.' He ran from one side to the other shouting at the distant view and laughing at the town, just like Toytown, far below us. The people too were like little dollies walking with the help of a puppet string. The river snaked away between the high green banks feeling its way gently into the countryside.

I was dragged back to the present by the sight of Mam gathering up her bag, and her cigarettes and matches, and turning off the gas-fire all in one wind-milling movement.

'Come on you two. Time we all got to bed. You might be able to sleep in, but I can't. You should really get to bed earlier anyway. Specially when you get back to school.'

As we padded up to bed behind her, I thought that if going to bed earlier meant that I would have to miss that last hour with her, then I would be going to bed late forever. I had gone asleep in afternoon school before, and I would again.

* * *

'Well, where did you get them?'

We had settled down in our beds, on either side of the narrow room, and had waited for the familiar sound of heavy breathing from the other side of the wooden partition. Mam was asleep.

'It doesn't really matter, does it?' Teddy's voice

was muffled by the bedclothes. We always pulled them right up round our ears to keep the cold of the room out.

'I just want to know.'

'I found them on that wasteland beside the gas works. There was one of those tramp signs on the ground, so I dug down and there they were.'

'Daft. Don't believe you. Those books have never been under the ground. Go on. Tell me where you really got them.'

'Well, I went down the town to that pub behind Woolworths. Called The Grapes, you know. Porky said he knew a way in, round the back.'

'Porky,' I said, disgustedly.

'I don't know what you're bothered about him for! He's alright! Anyway, we climbed over the fence into the back yard. Lots of sheds and barrels and things. So we had a scrounge around. The books were in a big tin trunk.'

'Was it alright to bring them?'

'Yeah. Course it is. They wouldn't have been chucked out there in that old shed to rot, if the people wanted them, would they?'

I put my hand under the bed and felt the cardboard box now stuffed full of the precious books. Still there. I turned over and pulled the blankets over my head. Maybe it wasn't right to take them, but who would know, anyway?

The next day, Porky called for Teddy before we had got up, so he had to sit in the kitchen and wait while Teddy got himself a sandwich. It was well after ten o'clock, but we never bothered about getting up early during the holidays. Mam always got herself out at half-past seven without waking us. I was making the tea and cutting myself a sandwich, when Porky actually spoke to me.

'How old are you, then?'

'Ten, nearly.'

'Did you like the books we got you?' He was looking at me quite kindly, and I was just wishing he'd pretend I wasn't there again.

'Yes, they're smashing,' I said, biting hard on my sandwich. 'A bit old, though.'

'What are you going to do with them?'

'Read them, I suppose.' I chewed the sandwich and there was a silence. 'I might start a library, just to lend to the other kids, who're not in the big library'. As soon as I said that I could have bit my tongue off. This was an idea I had had inside my head for a long time, and I saw the two boys grinning at each other as I said it. I picked up my cup and slammed into the living room.

Not long after that, I heard the back door bang, and they were gone. Normally I would have been mad at Teddy going off again, but this morning I breathed a sigh of relief. I dashed upstairs and got the cardboard box full of books. I spread all the books out on the hearthrug, so I could have a good look at every one. I lit the gas fire to dry them out, and began to read the one with the most pictures.

I spent the rest of the day reading them, and turning the pages over to make sure they dried out properly. I made some paste out of flour and water and stuck clean pages out of an old diary on to the front page of each book. That would do for the date, although I would have to write it with a pencil, as I didn't have a date-stamp. By half-past three, my library was ready.

I set the books in two neat rows on the couch and went out in search of customers. The only people playing in the street were the Stretter twins, two thinfaced girls who were ten and Jonty Baron who was twelve, but as my Mam always said, not quite all there. He came as soon as I asked him, but the twins had to be enticed with the promise of some icing-sugar-balls, which I could make pretty quickly when they were looking at the books.

Jonty eagerly set about turning all the books over and busily looked at one upside down. The twins picked up a book each, then put it down, and demanded together. 'Where's them sugar-balls?'

I dashed into the kitchen to make them, listening hard to their squeals and Jonty's low voice as he chattered to himself, as I did so. I came back in with a handful of balls, which the twins grabbed straight away. Then they dashed for the door. Shiela Stretter, the taller and meaner one turned round. 'We didn't think much of them tatty old books. Some library!' I could hear them shriek-ing and laughing, as they ran down the street eat-ing my sugar-balls. I could have killed them.

Now Jonty was coming towards me, showing me the book with the brightest pictures, my own particular favourite. 'You like this one, Jonty?'

He nodded eagerly.

'You like to take it home?'

He grinned very broadly.

'Well, I will put the date in, and you can take it home.' I printed the date in my best numbers. 'Mind, you must bring it back this week.' He nod-ded again, but I knew he would have forgotten all this by tomorrow. I had played with Jonty before.

*   *   *

Teddy came in, ten minutes before Mam was due.

'Where have you been?'

'All over.'

'You didn't come in for dinner!'

'I had some at Porky's house. There were so many there they didn't notice one extra. Don't you tell Mam, though. What have you been do-ing?'

'Sorting the books out, and drying them. I read one of them right through.'

'I told old Porky you'd like them. Are they back in the box? I don't want Mam seeing them.'

I nodded, and got on with my jobs. There were still the breakfast pots to wash. I moved round Teddy, who was lying full length on the couch, and wondered if he was going out again tonight.

*   *   *

As I had half expected, Porky did turn up again about seven o'clock. This time he actually came in and sat. He shared a cup of pop with Teddy before they went out again. While he was in, Porky talked to me a bit, but I only mumbled my answers, and just went on with the picture I was drawing in the back of an old accounts book, that my Mam had whipped from the factory.

When the door closed behind them this time, I didn't feel sad at all. I breathed a sigh of relief and went upstairs for the cardboard box. Downstairs again, I spread the books out again and chose one called *The Honour of Mabel Carstairs*. It was about this lovely girl who had a nanny and a mother and father and many Aunts. She was good to everyone and never told a lie, and everyone loved her.

It took me three chapters to discover that the Nanny was not her Grandma, but a sort of servant who did everything for her. Round our place lots of kids call their Grandma Nan, and I never thought you would call a servant that.

I had just got to this spot where Mabel is taking

a basket of food and a parcel of clothes to some very poor children who lived close by, when the door smashed open and the boys came bouncing in again. The draught from the door nearly blew me off my chair and I yelled at the boys to shut it.

Teddy had a cardboard box under his arm, and Porky was carrying a sack, or something covered by a sack. Teddy put the box carefully beside me, saying, 'Got you some more of them books seeing as you like them so much.' I tipped them out and compared them with the ones I already had. They were pretty much the same, only with different titles, and two had a bonnier binding in a sort of rich red. Rich! That's how I felt, with all these books!

'Hey, but look here.' Porky exclaimed, to both of us, I think. He had put his sack on the table and was carefully disentangling a box from its folds. It was a greeny black tin, rather ordinary I thought.

'That's not up to much,' I said.

'Doesn't look much, but it rattled, so we thought we would bring it away to have a look at it.'

Teddy went out the back and came back with one of Mam's old baking knives. 'This should do it.'

They poked and prised, and at last pulled off the rusty hinges, having given up trying to force the padlock. Porky picked up what looked like a dirty cloth bag with a drawstring top. He loosened off

the string, and tipped out a coin into his other hand. It was thick and heavy looking and much bigger than any coin I had ever seen. It was a dirty yellow colour. It looked like gold to me.

Teddy grabbed it and rubbed it on the sleeve of his jumper. 'Yer bloke. It's gold. It's got to be gold!' He was jumping up and down and his eyes were popping out as though they just couldn't believe what they saw. He flipped the coin over, and it hit my outstretched hand with a heavy thump. I rubbed the face with my thumb feeling the clean sharp outline. It was like a brand new coin, but the face on the front was not our King.

'Must be old, like the books,' he said.

'Maybe even older,' added Porky. By now, he had a whole pile of coins on the table. We put them in rows. There were a few different King's faces on, and one or two queens, and the coins weren't all as big as the first one. There were two cases lined with blue velvet, with sets of coins in. The outsides of the cases looked faded and old, but inside the velvet looked nearly new. It was blackish blue like the sky on a summer night.

'These must be worth a mint,' said Porky importantly.

'Yes. We're rich,' shouted Teddy leaping up and down. 'Must be worth thousands of pounds, I bet. Just think what we can do.' We were all grinning like those circus clowns.

'I could buy a bike with three speeds,' shouted Porky.

'Yes, and one of those sets of cycling gear,' added Teddy, 'and maybe a stove and a storm-lantern for the den.'

'Yes,' I shrieked, 'and I could buy some books, new ones, and some shelves to keep them on.'

'A car for Mam to go to work, and a new coat instead of that old red one . . .' put in Teddy.

'And new shoes,' I crowed.

Then I sat down with a thump.

'But it isn't really ours,' I said sadly.

'Not ours?' shouted Teddy. 'We found it!'

'It's pinching.'

'It's no different from finding the books. It's only that the coins might be worth more.'

That's what had been niggling me for the last two days. I wasn't happy about the books, either, much as I loved them. But, if the coins were stolen, then the books were stolen, and that was that. I thought hard about that cardboard box under my bed, happily full of books, my own special treasure.

'You'll have to take them back,' I said stubbornly, 'keeping things like that is stealing. What if the cops find out?'

'How could they? No one knew the coins were there, or they wouldn't have chucked them out like that would they?'

I thought again about the police. They were

pretty clever, and Mam's biggest nightmare was that we should get into trouble. The boys were looking at me and slyly fingering the coins, dropping them from one hand to the other.

'Look,' I said desperately, 'you can take the books back, every one, if you like. I tell you what, I'll even take the books back myself, if only you'll take them coins back. You'll get into such trouble,' I groaned.

Porky was suddenly smiling a funny smile. 'Alright,' he said cockily, 'if you take the books back yourself, on your own, we'll take the coins back.'

I shuddered at the thought of those dark back alleys behind the high street. 'Yes,' I said, cool as I could. 'Alright, you take the coins, and I'll take the books. When?'

They argued a bit with each other, then gave in. 'Tonight'd be best,' said Teddy. 'After our Mam's gone to sleep. Can you meet us near Woolworths about a quarter to twelve, Porky?'

'Alright. I suppose so.' You could tell Porky was narked. He didn't want me to do it.

We hid the coins and the books in the cardboard box with the other books. I went to put on the kettle for Mam's pot of tea. Porky went, after having a long chat with Teddy in the lobby. The last thing I heard him say was 'Don't girls make you sick?'

For the first time ever I died for Mam to go straight to bed when she came in. I hoped that tonight she would be that bit extra tired. What happened was, that she stayed up later than usual, and we didn't even go to bed till half past eleven.

*   *   *

We lay in bed with our clothes on, till Mam dropped off to sleep. It seemed ages before it was safe to move, but the old travel clock on Teddy's table still only showed twenty to twelve. I lifted an old rucksack, that had been my Dad's, on to the bed, and packed that with as many books as I could. There were still some left in the cardboard box. I was weighed down with the haversack and couldn't see how I could carry the others.

'I'll take them.' Teddy was already stuffing them into a carrier.

I sighed with relief. 'Thanks.' Teddy was wrapping the tin up in its sack, and tying it with one of the bits of string from his collection. We had not put on the light, for fear of waking Mam, but the light from the streetlamp was streaming through the window, and we could easy see our hands as we scrabbled with the books and the tin.

We crept downstairs in our socks, pausing on the steps that creaked, to make sure Mam didn't stir. The rucksack was pulling me backwards, so hard that I felt I would fall over backwards if someone just touched me. But I didn't say anything to Teddy. I had said I was taking them books back, and meant it. I would make them boys do something I wanted. Especially that Porky.

We let the latch down gently as we crept out. I had never been out that late before, and the black sky beyond the streetlamps seemed extra black, and the narrow houses seemed to rear extra high. It was cold and the lamps found their shiny reflection in the wet surface of the street. We walked on tiptoe, but could still hear the faint echo of our steps bouncing back at us from the high walls on the opposite side of the narrow street.

I was quickly making my way to the main street, when Teddy suddenly grabbed me. I nearly fell backwards on to the heavy rucksack with shock. 'What do you think you're doing,' I whispered fiercely.

'Can't go down the main street. Coppers. Walk up and down all night. Have to go down the backs.'

I shook. I had had to steel myself to the thought of going down the main street in the middle of the night, but the thought of those back alleys, without even streetlights, scared me rigid.

'You scared?' muttered Teddy.

'Course I'm not,' I lied, and to prove it I started down the back without him. I could have cried with relief when he caught me up, and grabbed my arm. I don't know even now, whether the grab was to give me courage, or to stop himself being frightened.

Some sections of the back streets were so dark

that we found ourselves feeling down the walls. Once we happened to scrape across a gate, and a great barking and howling was set up, by some dog that we roused from sleep. Black as it was, we ran for a whole minute without the help of the wall. I fell down and Teddy dragged me to my feet. The only sounds were our sobbing breaths and the bark of the dog growing steadily fainter.

Twice we heard loud arguing conversations, of people just coming home, but in each case they were too fully occupied to notice two silent figures gliding by. By now I knew Teddy was as frightened as I was, and we ended up holding each others hands like we had when we were much smaller. We really needed to to guide each other.

'Nearly there now.' The big storehouse doors of Woolworths shone faintly red in the wet reflection from distant streetlamps. 'Just round the corner.'

We turned the corner and went slam into Porky. 'Just going home, I was.' He growled.

'Sorry we're late,' gasped Teddy, 'but our Mam just wouldn't go to bed.' I could have killed him for apologising to that fat boy. We didn't need Porky. We could easy have put the stuff back on our own.

'Never mind,' said Porky. 'Lets get on with it.'

He turned to look at the high wall which must have led to the back of the Grapes. I tugged at Teddy's coat. 'I can't climb that.' He turned to Porky.

'Our May can't climb that wall.'

'Well she'll have to. We agreed. We're only putting the coins back if she puts the books back.'

'I can take them in.' said Teddy.

'That doesn't count.' Porky muttered fiercely.

It was just like Porky to turn awkward, but in a way I was pleased. I would find a way. I didn't need any silly boys to help. I wandered along the lane a bit. The high wall gave way to an equally high fence. My fingers ran along the fence as I walked. One of the laths of wood moved as my hand passed over it. Just what I wanted. I pulled it a bit and it came away as though it were fixed in place with plasticine.

'I can get through here.' The boys came over.

'Pretty good, pretty good.' Porky seemed quite impressed. I unhooked myself from the rucksack and pushed it through the narrow space.

'I'll get through here,' I whispered. 'You go your way and I'll see you inside.'

'Right,' said Teddy, and Porky nodded.

I squeezed myself painfully through the narrow space, and found myself, and my rucksack, in an equally tiny space between the fence and what looked like a shed with a steep roof. I made my way to the open end of the space, dragging the rucksack behind me. I couldn't have got it up on my back, never mind carry it there.

I found myself in a long narrow cobbled yard. The massive gable end of the pub dominated the other end of the yard. There were still lights on downstairs, and I could hear the tinkle of glasses. They must still be cleaning up. There were stone outhouses all the way down the yard, with big wooden doors, and two wooden sheds. There was the small one past which I had just squeezed, and a much bigger one on the other side.

Teddy jumped lightly on to the yard beside me. Porky was on top of the wall, standing very black against the sky. He threw down the box, which Teddy caught with a grunt, and put carefully on the cobbles. Then came the tattered carrier with the rest of my books in, and then Porky himself.

We all stood still and quiet for a minute, just to get our breaths back. Then I walked over to the large shed. 'This the place?' I whispered. Teddy was beside me.

'Yeah, but be careful. The door's heavy.'

He cautiously lifted the latch and heaved the door outwards.

The inside of the shed was piled high with boxes and chests and piles of things from faded piles of clothes to furniture. Porky pointed to a tea chest. That's where the books were. The rough lid was not fixed on, so I put it on the floor. The chest was still half full, so without looking I just tipped my precious books in. Then, tipping up the carrier, I put the rest of the books on top. I turned to Porky, 'Now you,' I demanded. He had got the box out of its sacking, and was just about to raise the lid of a tin trunk in another corner, when Teddy said quietly 'Cave!' He had been standing in the doorway of the shed.

Porky quietly placed the box on to the lid of the trunk, and we both crept over to the door. We looked out in the direction that Teddy was pointing. At the spot where the two boys had climbed over. There was a hand on the wall, and another hand was scrabbling to find a secure hold beside it.

'Come on,' Porky breathed, and I found myself dragged along the wall to a spot where barrels, some the size of a man, were standing beside the wall. We squeezed into the space behind them and sat very still. By peering through a space between two barrels we could still see what was happening.

The hands had been followed by a head, and one man had dropped lightly to the ground. Another man quickly followed. I felt icy-cold but there was sweat running right down my back.

*   *   *

A shot of light spilled over from the lamp in the street outside. It shone on the side of the shed we had just left, picking out the grain of the old wood shed and making the dusty windows look like dead eyes. The two men moved into this beam of half light so we could see them more clearly. They were both quite tall but one was much heavier than the other, and wore glasses that glinted in the light from the streetlamp.

The thinner man had very bushy hair that stood away from his face and only seemed to grow from halfway back on his head. His forehead gleamed, making a set with the other fellow's glasses. We

listened to their whispered talk, jammed as we were, only a foot or so away from them, in the shadow behind the barrels.

'Still a bit of action in there. Must be clearing up. Best hang about for a while.' Whispered the big man. The other man was messing about with the door of the shed. He lifted it up, and lifted it open without making any noise. 'In here.' He whispered.

They slipped in and pulled the door behind them without actually shutting it.

'The box!' Porky was beside the door, his ear close to the crack. In a minute he was beside us again. 'They've found the box,' he reported. 'Gonna take it with them when they've done the job.'

'The job!' My head bobbed up, only to be pushed down by Porky's rough hand.

'Keep down you nit. They're going to pinch money from the pub. Just waiting for the people to go to bed.'

'We'd better tell the pub man,' growled Teddy.

'Can't.' Porky dismissed the idea. 'The cops'd be asking why we were here, and if these blokes were pinching, what was we doing out here in the middle of the night?'

We all crouched down in silence. What Porky said was true. Who would have believed our story, and even if they did, it wasn't such a good story anyway. They'd just say we were up to no good ourselves out at that time of night. And why hadn't we reported the coins when we first found them?

There was a breath of movement from across the yard. The men were coming out of the shed. The big thickset one was carrying our box, and the other one, once the shed door was fixed, reached into his pocket, pulled out something, and his hands went to his head. It was a stocking. I had read that they sometimes used them as masks, but I still gasped at the horrific effect it had on his appearance.

The bottom half of his body was lost in the shadow of the wall we had just climbed. There was just his shoulders and the awful squashed plasticine of his face under the stocking. The fuzzy arc of his hair was gone, and the mesh obliterated even the gleam of his eyes.

I started to shake, and it was only Porky's hard grasp on my shoulders and the way he breathed 'Steady!' that stopped me screaming out. The men were whispering and making gestures with their hands. I prayed that they would get on with whatever they were going to do, and we could just get out, right away from this awful place and out of the dreadful night.

The men crept up the yard away from us without a sound. I could hear gasps from both sides of me as the boys began to relax and breathe normally again. We waited for them to vanish. They opened the door easily enough, just used a key, from a ring which rustled in the quiet, then pushed hard. We heard a kind of grinding noise that could have been a bolt breaking, and a gasp of satisfaction from one of the men.

*   *   *

It took us a minute to realise that one of the men had vanished, and to our horror that the one without the mask was leaning casually against the doorpost with our tin box under his arm. He was doing something for his mate, that I had done many times for Teddy when he was up to one of his many tricks. He was keeping Cavey. Watching for trouble.

There was a breath of a moan from behind me and Porky whispered, his voice as light as the breezes that were blowing at the eaves of the pub. 'We'll just have to wait till they go away.' We couldn't even relax, and wriggle our toes, as any movement would have drawn the man's attention.

Time went by slowly as we sat there feeling the damp seep into our clothes, not daring to move an inch. Then there was a noise from inside, and we heard a grunt rather than a shout as the man inside called to the man outside. He ducked inside the door and vanished, and Porky whispered 'Right!'

In two seconds I was across the yard and had wriggled through the crack in the fence. Teddy nearly fell on top of me as Porky hoyked him over the wall, but took a bit longer to scramble over himself. Without even consulting each other, we crossed the narrow back lane and made our way down an even narrower one leading off from it. Halfway down that, we all stopped to get our breaths back, leaning against a wall.

We stayed there a minute, gasping without speaking, and when I felt the air going evenly into my lungs again, I set away down the back again. A hand pulled me back, by the forgotten rucksack on my shoulders.

'Hang on a minute. Where do you think you're going?' It was Porky in a mean grim sort of voice.

'Home, where do you think.' I turned to Teddy for support, but he was just gasping still, against the wall. I had always been able to run faster and further than him, in spite of being younger.

'What about the men? They're off to rob that pub?' Porky was arguing with me as though Teddy wasn't there.

'If we go to get somebody, they'll know we've been. Don't you see?' I was sick of the whole thing and just wanted to get home.

'We needn't get anybody. We could just follow them to see where they go, so we'll know where our box is. Mebbe get it back sometime. What do you think, Ted?'

Teddy looked at me, frowning a bit as he still leaned against the wall. 'I don't know.'

'Don't say you're scared!'

'It's not that, just, well we might get into bother.'

'Don't you care about the treasure, then?'

Teddy stood away from the wall, and began to rub the top of his legs. 'I suppose it wouldn't do any harm just to find where they take it to.'

'Teddy!' I don't know whether I cried or wailed or shouted, but it must have come out pretty loud.

'Shush, kid. You can go home if you don't want to come with me.'

I opened my mouth to say I daren't go home on my own, back up those back alleys, then shut it again. 'Well, if that's what you want to do, I'll help,' was all I said. I didn't say I would feel safer with them, but I would.

We crept back to the corner, keeping the back fence of the Grapes in view. I unhitched myself from the rucksack, and sat on it, glad at least for the few minutes rest. Teddy shoved me along and sat beside me, and with him so close, we were both a bit warmer. Porky kept watch, peering round the corner with his back flat against the wall so as not to be seen. It occurred to me that had we just stood there and watched normally, the men wouldn't have noticed. Who'd expect to see three kids out at this time of night?

I didn't say what I thought, as it would probably have sounded a bit sneery, just like those twins had sounded about my library. Teddy was nudging me. He held out his big pocket watch for me to see. It was the big silver one he had ticed from our Mam, and had managed to get working again, by some miracle. The watch said a quarter to one. I had thought it must be about three o'clock. It seemed like a hundred years since we had sneaked out of the house on what I had thought would be a bit of a joke. I stretched my legs and thought of the thick army blanket on my bed, at home.

'Wrrst'. It was half a whistle, half a shout from Porky. We slowly got up, making as little noise as we could. Peeping round the corner, we caught sight of the second, slighter man jumping down from the wall. He had pulled off his mask and his bushy hair was flying free.

He picked up a sack that he must have thrown to the ground. His mate, who was still clutching the box, helped him to get it on his shoulders. They both set away walking quietly, but with some speed, in the direction that led away from us.

Porky turned round. 'You two ready?' We both nodded. 'Well come on. Be quiet and keep your distance, but try to keep them in sight.' Then he set off, and we two followed on behind him like a pair of little sheep. . .

*   *   *

The route they took was quite complicated. It was obvious that they were as keen to avoid the main thoroughfares as we were. Even at this time of night the police made their regular patrols. At one point the men had to cross the main street and they were very cautious. They stood together in a shop doorway, and then the heavy one crossed over. The other one waited several seconds before he followed suit. This way, I suppose, if the police caught one, they could easily miss the other one.

'Do the same,' muttered Teddy. He went first, and I waited, then I went. Porky followed twenty seconds later. He seemed to be floodlit by the big streetlights, and his shadow was twice as big as himself. I was secretly pleased at this little exercise, as it was Teddy who had given the orders, and not the insufferable Porky.

The men were swiftly getting themselves swallowed up in the narrow complex of streets and back-alleys, so we had to hurry a bit to make up for lost time. They were walking quite quickly, which meant that we kept having to break into a run. We ran from corner to corner, stopping on one corner till they had turned the next one. This was not difficult as the streets were so short.

Then we turned a corner and they were gone. We could see the whole of the street into which they had only just turned. The pavement, the single street lamps at each end, shining on the cobbles like a thousand tiny hills. The street was empty. We retreated back round the corner. I felt muddled, and very tired, too weary even to think about those silly men and where they had gone.

'They've vanished.' I stated.

'Don't talk rubbish,' whispered Teddy. 'Men don't vanish. They must have gone into one of these houses. They must live here.'

'Right.' Porky's voice was full of approval. 'The thing is, which one?'

I saw a glimmer of light in a house just three doors from the end, then it vanished. 'There was a light across at that one, just a second ago. The third from the end.'

Teddy flitted across the road like a shadow, and was back in a minute. 'It's number five,' he peered up, trying to make out the name of the street that was just above the point where the light hit the wall from the nearby lamp. 'I think it says Baker Street.'

Porky laughed quietly, then whispered. 'Now what can we do? We know where the money is, we know where the gold is, but if we tell the cops they'll have us in for sure, and more'n likely have us up for nickin' it.'

We stood quiet and helpless. Then Teddy cleared his throat and I knew he was going to say something sensible. 'Best sleep on it I should think.'

'Good idea,' said Porky, thankfully, turning back towards home. I fell into step with them, mutely grateful that they had decided to halt their adventuring for a while. Any more, and I felt I'd have just sat down and bubbled like a baby.

We trudged back along the streets much more slowly than we had followed the men. We were worn out, but still remembered to be cautious in the area of the main street. Porky left us on the edge of the estate that bordered on to the wood, and we went with ever slower steps towards our little street and our little house. We crept in like mice, suddenly fearing that Mam had woken up for some strange reason. But everything was just as we had left it. I threw myself on to the bed, and pulled over the blanket, without even bothering to take off my jeans and sweater. Teddy went through his usual routine of folding things neatly over a chair, and I was practically off to sleep when he was clambering on to his bed. I was half into a dream when I heard him say, 'You were pretty good tonight for a kid just ten, May. Not bad.' And I drifted off to sleep with a heart as high as a feather.

*   *   *

I was on that ship again, but this time Porky was steering, moving a great thing like a wheel from side to side. The sea was washing over the side and I had this beer tankard in my hand. I kept lifting the water up and throwing it out, lifting it up and throwing it out. The sea kept washing in a bucketful, for every tankard I got rid of. I kept looking up to Porky and shouting 'we can't do it, we can't do it!' He just turned and turned the wheel and looked right ahead.

This made me so mad that I began to bang the tankard on the wood side of the boat. But the glass didn't shatter as it should have done and my desperate efforts made no more sound than if the tankard were made from sponge.

I sat up in bed. There was someone who kept banging, banging on the door. I could hear the letterbox rattling furiously. I leapt out of bed, and reached automatically for my clothes, before I looked down and realised that they were still on. My jeans had a thousand creases, and the jumper was halfway up my back. I pulled it down and shook Teddy.

'Someone at the door, Teddy.'

He just groaned and rolled over, and I had to go myself.

I was at the turn on the stairs on our little back staircase before I remembered what had happened last night. The box! The thieves! Creeping about in the frightening dark! I stood still, and clung to the bannister. The door was rattling even more, and I could hear a muffled voice. Even through the letterbox, and the space of the big room and the kitchen, I recognised Porky's deep tones. I hurried on.

Porky nearly fell in as I unbolted the door. 'You lot must be dead. I've been standing here knocking for ten minutes.'

I let him past me but didn't say anything. He went in the room and sat on the couch. I could feel his eyes on me as I walked round to light the gas fire. The gas gave that quiet plop as I stopped its hissing with a match flame. I threw the match down with the rest, on the hearth.

'Where's Ted then?'

'He's asleep. Couldn't wake him. Its after that late night.'

'Hey, yes, but its past eleven now. Enough sleep for any man.'

I sniffed. 'Well you try. I couldn't do it.'

He went through to the kitchen and stood at the bottom of the stairs, and bellowed, 'Teddy! Are you dead, man? It's past eleven.'

Straight away there were sounds of movement upstairs. I put the kettle on, and lit the grill for the toast. Teddy appeared on the stairs and sat down beside Porky on the bottom step. He bent down to fasten his shoelaces.

'I can't believe it's happened. I mean those men and the box and being out there in the middle of it all.' His voice was excited and you wouldn't have known he had been asleep a few minutes ago.

'And that mask!' I shuddered as I put a spoonful of cocoa into each of three cups.

'Yeah, pretty weird!' agreed Porky.

We all sat round the table and ate the toast and drank the cocoa. Porky took charge. He was so obviously the boss that it was queer to me, having always had to do what Teddy said.

'The thing is,' said Porky, 'what do we have to do next?'

'Do?' echoed Teddy. 'Why, we can't do nothing. If we tell anybody about all we saw, they'll know we were there and then they'll ask questions, won't they just?'

Then all we could hear was ourselves chewing away at the toast, and slurping the cocoa.

Porky broke the silence by crashing his cocoa cup on to the table.

'I think we should find some way of talking to the landlord without seeing the police.'

'Couldn't do that,' muttered Teddy, 'he'd just report us to the police anyway, and we would be right up to our necks in it then.'

'Yeah. But if he was very keen to get it back, he might help us to keep out of the cops' way.' I could see that Porky was enjoying all this. Loving all the plotting and scheming. He didn't worry about getting into trouble like I did. Maybe his mam didn't mind quite so much as mine would. I put my oar in.

'We'd have to tell him about the tin box, you know, not just about his takings.'

Porky made sounds of protest, but Teddy butted in. 'She's right you know!'

Porky folded his lips tight for a minute or two, then relaxed and gave us quite a friendly grin that showed a gap in his teeth at one side. 'I suppose you're right. Even so I'd just like them blokes to get nabbed because it seems as though they've stole our box. Even if it really is old Bockwith's. If we told him about the box, as well as where his money's gone to, he might be pretty pleased and wouldn't even think of telling the cops.'

It was hard to argue with this, and Teddy gave in straight away. 'Okay. We'll tell him. But we'll have to find out first if we can trust him.'

'No good me going,' Porky said gloomily. 'He caught me taking some empty bottles from his yard once, and said if he caught me in there again, he would have me up.'

'Then I'll go,' said Teddy straight away, not scared at all. I was proud of him. Porky looked at him frowning.

'Don't think that would do, Ted. Old Bockwith don't like boys at all, they say. They say he keeps a shotgun under the bar, loaded with blanks of course, to keep boys off tormenting him.'

'How's that?' Teddy, and me as well, were puzzled.

'Well he's a big man, but he had one very short leg, and he walks right over on that side. So he gets a bit tormented by some boys. They call him Peggy or Lefty and run after him.' From the angelic look on Porky's face he never did cruel things like that, but I bet he had been there, yelling away with the worst of them. 'So,' he concluded, 'I think its best if May goes.'

'May—But she's just a girl, and only a kid.' Teddy was furious, I could tell by the way he kept throwing his hair back.

'Aye. But look at her last night. She was great. Couldn't of done better if she had been a lad. Although she is just a kid.'

At this I went red as a brick oven, and felt as though somebody had given me a medal. Teddy was as pleased at this praise as I had been, and retired from the argument.

'Would you like to do it, May?' He turned to me. They both looked at me as though I were some insect on a glass plate, about to do something interesting. To go to the pub and talk to the man was the last thing I wanted to do, but I was trapped. If Porky had tried to force me, I would just have refused point blank. But the way he had praised me, I couldn't do anything else but agree.

'Alright. I'll do it.'

Porky stood up and brushed the crumbs from his

pullover.

'Good kid. No good going today. The place'll be crawling with people, and cops. Mebbe some time tomorrow.'

I started to clear away, and Teddy stood up and leaned against the wall where Porky stood. 'I think we should go down there and hang around a bit. See what's happening, and what the action is.'

'Great idea,' said Porky. 'We'll see how the land lies.'

I discovered much later that Porky was as big a reader as I was, and often talked like you would read in one of those adventure books. Teddy looked round the room. 'No need for you to come, May. Plenty for you to be doing here.' I hadn't expected to be invited, so being put off like that was no surprise. Even so, I still felt mad, and for the first time in my life felt annoyed at being a girl. I crashed the pots into the sink, and by the time I had finished crashing, they had gone.

*   *   *

There was a note from Mam on the mantlepiece. 'May, love. You were sleeping the sleep of the dead when I went out so I hadn't the heart to wake you. Can you get some eggs and sausage and bread with this money? And you can get something nice for you and Teddy as well. Sweets or something.'

I always had the messages to do. Mam always

said she could rely on me to do what she said, as Teddy often forgot, being busy with other things. I usually liked to do it anyway as I could walk around the town with a purpose, and feel as though I were really somebody.

Today I was pleased to go as it would stop me thinking about the night before. If I'd had to sit around the house thinking, without even the books to take my mind off it, I think I'd have gone mad.

I picked up Mam's big shopping bag, and slung Teddy's scarf round my neck. The house was cold enough inside, I remember thinking, so what the heck will it be like outside? I walked along the street past Old Mrs. Miles who was cemented to her doorpost as usual. Teddy swore she only left it to sleep, as she was always there. But I'd seen her having her dinner at her table beside the window.

I soon reached main street, and went into the first butchers' for the sausage. Mam had told me never to go there, as the prices were sky high, but I always went, because Mr. Milroy, who served, was so nice. Today it was only sausages I wanted, but he selected them with care, and only wrapped them up when he was quite satisfied that they were the ones I really wanted. It was while he was wrapping them that I heard some conversation between two women waiting to be served.

'I see the Grapes was busted into. They say four hundred pounds was took.'

'Yes. I did hear there was four of them, all with

masks and big coshes. Old man Bockwith disturbed them, but not before they got their hands on his money. Four hundred! Who would think he would have that much on tap. Sly old devil.'

I snatched the parcel of sausage off Mr. Milroy and ran out of the shop with my face as red as beet-root, I had reached Woolworths which was much further down, before I realised I hadn't paid for the sausages. I would have to call on the way back, but those women would be gone by then.

I had hoped to see Teddy or even Porky down the street, but although I hung around a bit, and even went into Jane's Kozy Cafe for a drink of pop, there was no sign of them. I could only think that they had spent the day at Porky's, and didn't want me hanging around.

I was sitting in the Cafe, drinking my own pop, and staring out of the window when there was a clatter beside me. This girl had been carrying an icecream in a glass over to one of the scrubbed tables beside the window. She had not noticed Mam's big shopping bag lying beside me, and she went flying. The ice went flying through the air and landed with a splintering crash on the floor, the girl was sprawled behind it with her legs in the air and showing her blue check knickers, and my shopping was scattered all round my feet.

'Hey!' I leapt up ready to tell her off for being clumsy, but even as I was jumping up I remembered that my shopping bag had been right in the

middle of the aisle, and it was really my fault. I went over to help her up.

'Sorry about that. I never seem to look where I'm going.' She had a nice voice, with some kind of accent I didn't recognise. It wasn't exactly posh but it was different.

The fat woman from behind the counter had come bustling out, moaning and complaining, but cleaning up the splintered glass. The girl bent to help me pick up my shopping.

'I am sorry. Seems as if the bread's got a bit dirty.'

'That's okay,' I said, 'I'll toast that bit and no-body'll notice.'

We both laughed at the unsuspecting victim who would eat the blemished bread, and the girl sat quite naturally at my table when I sat down to finish my pop. I took a quick drink.

'Look,' I offered. 'I can get you another ice. My Mam gave me some money to buy something for my brother, but he's out somewhere, and he'll know no different anyway.'

'That's very kind, but I don't really feel like another, to tell you the truth.'

She smoothed some creases out of the red wool skirt she was wearing under a thick dark blue jacket. She had a very brown foreign looking skin and thick black shiny hair that was looped up in two bunches, one beside each ear. They looked almost like snaky black earrings. She broke my stare.

'Alright then, I will have one, if you really want me to.'

When I brought back the ice, she smiled and set about eating it at once. As she scooped spoonful after spoonful into her mouth I wondered why on earth I had spent Teddy's money on her. She was strange-looking though.

'Do you not come from round here?'

'No. I am staying here with my grandfather, to go to school. My father has gone to Singapore with the army and they thought it would be better for me to stay here to go to school.'

'Your grandfather? But there aren't any er——'

'Foreigners? Ah well you see, I am not a foreigner. My father was born here in this town and is as British as your Yorkshire pudding. So I am British. My mother was Italian though, which is why I don't look the part, and I spend much time with my Italian grandparents near Milano, so I don't sound much British either.'

'Which school will you go to, then?' I suddenly wished it was mine, then we could be real friends.

'Caldwell Road Grammar School I think its called. A place big and red bricks.'

'Oh.' I was disappointed. 'You must be older than me, though you a'nt much bigger. I'm still at Wearbreak Juniors.'

She must have known what I was thinking, and she frowned, 'That doesn't mean we cannot be friends, does it?'

I thought about Porky and Teddy. 'No, I don't suppose it does. What's your name?'

'Maria Barbara, a huge name I'm afraid. After my two grandmothers I'm told.'

'My name's just May. May Wintersgill.'

'That's nice and short. I like that. May.'

She scooped up the last spoonful. 'How would it be if you came to my grandfather's to play with me?'

'I don't know. I have things to do for my mam.'

'You could just come for half an hour. It's not far from here.'

I stood up, pulled my jumper down, and wrapped the thick scarf round my neck. 'Alright then. Just half an hour.'

Maria talked excitedly as we walked up the street. 'My grandfather will be so pleased you are coming. I have been here nearly a week now, and he is always complaining I have no friends, and to stop moping around. You will like him May. He talks very severely, but he is really wonderfully kind and jolly.'

We turned down a sidestreet, walked a few yards, and Maria Barbara stopped. 'Here we are. Grandfather won't mind if we go through the front.'

I looked up and I could feel my blood turning to icy chunks in my veins. Creaking and swinging directly above my head was a faded old sign. It was mainly a scratchy yellow, but right in the middle was a bunch of what could have been small black balloons. Underneath, in faded gold lettering were the words, 'The Grapes.'

'You don't live here?' My voice was weak with panic.

'Yes I do. At least my Grandfather does, and I stay with him. Don't you like pubs, or something?'

'It's not that. It's that I—I—I've never been inside one before.'

'Oh, there's nothing frightening about it. They are a bit cold and smelly when they're empty. But when the people are in, they are very happy noisy places.'

Then, before I knew it, she had me inside. The place did smell funny. Not dirty, but just as though it was going bad. There were polished tiles on the floor, and little wooden tables and stools scattered around. Right along the far wall was the bar, twinkling with bottles and mirrors.

'Through here.'

Maria Barbara was opening up part of the bar to let us through. Going through felt nice. I had often wondered what it felt like to be behind the counter in a shop. It must be a bit like this.

The glass-paned door rattled as we went through to the room where they lived. The first thing that hit my eye was the huge flickering fire set in the opposite wall. It roared away in a big black iron range, its orange light reflected in the shining brass fender, and the brass handle on the door of the oven. There were two big couches at either side of

the fire, and a big dinner table on the near wall beside the door by which we'd entered.

We both rushed to the fire to get warmed through, and I was pleased at the friendly heat on my face, although my stomach was churning over at being right here in this vital place.

'I'll say one thing,' said Maria Barbara feelingly, 'that even though Grandfather is lovely and much kinder than my Milano grandparents, at least Italy was warm, and you didn't have to wear layers and layers of clothes to keep out the cold.' I said nothing, just kept rubbing my hands.

The door on the fireplace-wall opened, and a tall fat man came in, with black pants and black braces over a striped collarless shirt, and a black beret completely covering his head, so you couldn't see whether or not he had any hair.

'Back then, are you? Did you get me tobacco?'

Maria Barbara fished a small parcel from the pocket of her jacket. 'No change. You gave me the right money for that and an icecream.'

'Who's this, then. You got a new friend?'

'Yes. This is my friend May. She has come to play. I knocked her shopping basket over in the cafe.'

'She must be a good pal to take that sort of treatment. What's your other name May?'

'Wintersgill.'

'You're not Charlie Wintersgill's offspring?'

'My Dad's name was Charlie.'

'Killed in the war, in the desert?'

'Yes.'

'Well, yer bloke. Many a pint he's had in here when he was just a young bit o' lad. Great pal of your father's Maria Barbara. Got up to some scrapes together when they were young, I can tell you. Had many a telling off from me when they were young. Good lad, though. Straight as a die. Pity you lost him, love. Sorry about that.'

'I can't remember him, but my brother Teddy does, a bit.'

'Got a brother, have you? Like to meet him sometime. Your mother must be having a bit of a job, with two of you to look after.'

'She always says she manages.'

'I'm sure she does. Well! Must be off. You're welcome to stay. Nice for Maria Barbara to have some company.' So, he bustled out, and both of us relaxed.

I didn't stay long, as it was after four already. I looked at Maria Barbara's dolls and books, then said I just had to go. She made me promise to come the next morning.

I was in a hurry to get home, but not just because I had the tea to do, but also to tell Teddy about the extraordinary meeting I had had today with the owner of the coins and his grand-daughter.

Teddy was sitting beside the fire, poring over an old medical dictionary that Mam had kept from her student nurse days. It was open at one of those terrible pictures which show all the veins of the body like a congested river system.

'Hey kid, where've you been?'

'Where've you been?' I retorted.

'Been over Porky's playing some of his records. He's got some great new ones. We've been trying to think of what to do about last night, but couldn't figure what to do without getting into trouble ourselves.'

Then I told him about my day, how I had met Maria Barbara, and gone home to the Grapes with her. Teddy whistled. 'And I met Mr. Bockwith, who's Maria Barbara's Granda, and he isn't half nice. He knew our Dad, who was Maria Barbara's dad's best pal. I took a deep breath. 'I think we should tell him about everything.' Teddy snorted. 'Yes, well he was so nice, I'm sure he wouldn't get us in trouble with the police. And that way he'd know where to get his money back, and the gold coins that are his too.'

'I don't know.' He was very dubious. 'Mebbe we should talk to Porky about it.'

I fumed. 'Porky, you just ask him for permission to breathe, these days!' and I slammed into the kitchen and started unwrapping the sausages.

Mam came in pretty soon after that, and Teddy started asking her questions about veins in the body and what was the difference between veins and arteries. It was after tea, before I got in my bit about meeting Maria Barbara. Mam was very interested. 'Bockwith? I've heard your Dad mention a

74

George Bockwith, many a time. Great pals they were when they were young. Never met him myself, though. Met your Dad after George had gone to the army as a boy soldier. Fancy you knowing his girl!'

'Yes. Well I'm going there tomorrow to play.'

'Good. Nice you having your own friend, instead of having to hang around Teddy all the time.' She gave us both the knowing look. That was the funny thing about Mam. We never saw much of her, with her having to go out to work so much. We got most of our own way, and did just what we wanted, but now and then she would just do something to show she still had her hand on us, and knew by instinct most of what happened to us.

'Teddy's pals with Porky too.'

She looked from one to the other. 'Well, that's everybody suited then isn't it. By the way. A bit of bad news from my end. They're going on short work across the factory. Could be at least twenty of us losing jobs. Probably be looking round for another job, then.'

She was suddenly a bit downhearted, not like her usual cheerful self. Both Teddy and I knew how important it was that she should keep her job. It was important to us all, but neither of us could think of anything to say to her, to cheer her up. What would we do?

She was a bit late going down to the pub, that night being Friday. She always got a bit dressed up on a Friday night. She wore her best dress, always the same old black one, but she did look smart, with her pearl necklace and earrings to match. Because she was late going, she met Porky for the first time. He was a bit embarrassed and stood very straight.

'What school do you go to, then?'

'Caldwell Road Grammar. I'm in the first year.'

'Good lad,' said Mam with feeling, 'and you get your nose down and get some real work done. It's the only way to get on, and out of dumps like this. I'm always telling our Teddy.' Porky shuffled his feet and looked uncomfortable, and only relaxed when Mam had gone.

He looked at both of us. 'Well? Got any ideas about those thieves?' he asked.

'Yes,' I answered straight away. 'We have to go to The Grapes and tell Mr. Bockwith the truth.'

Porky snorted with disagreement, 'And go straight to the nick?'

'Don't be soft! I tell you I met him today. I went to the pub with this girl I met who's his grand-daughter. I tell you he was a lovely man, and he wouldn't lay us in if we told him exactly what happened.' Even as I said it, I wasn't absolutely sure. There were certain things grown-ups did 'For your own good', just to keep their own conscience clear.

Porky was opening his mouth to pour more scorn on what I suggested, when unbelievably, Teddy leapt to my defence.

'She could be right, Pork. We're gonna have to tell somebody about it, and why not the old man if we can get him on our side? He could make up some story to the cops, and they could still get his money back.'

'Well . . .' Porky began.

'That's settled, then. We'll go down in the morning and spill the beans. No good going tonight 'cause the pub'll be in full swing, it being Friday.'

'If you're too scared, I can go on my own,' I slyly put in.

'Scared? Don't talk daft!' yelled Porky, and threw one of Mam's old cushions at me. I knew then that Porky was a bit my friend, as well as Teddy's.

The boys stayed in that night, as it was so miserably rainy outside. It was quite friendly really. They worked their way through a big pile of comics that Porky had brought, and I sorted the washing for Mam to do in the morning, a job I did every Friday. As I separated the light things from the dark things, the thick things from the thin things, I just wondered whether we wouldn't end up in the nick tomorrow after all.

Mam howled the next day, when I said I wanted to go out. 'There's so much to do! How can I manage without you!' I knew this was half in fun, as she never really nagged, but I stood there uncertain of what to say next. I could hardly say, 'I'm going to save Teddy and me from jail.' Then she laughed.

'Oh, get away with you. Going to see your new friend are you? Go on then. Friends are like new plants. Have to be watered and kept sweet for the friendship to thrive. Get on!'

I rushed upstairs and got a clean pair of jeans and a clean sweater from the tea-chest that held my clothes. I put some polish on my shoes and combed my hair really tidy.

Mam watched with amusement. 'It can only be a good friend that would have such a good influence on you!'

I never said anything, just gave her a wave as I dashed outside, to join Teddy and Porky who were on the doorstep. It only took us five minutes to reach the Grapes, and Porky pushed the bell that was at the top of the door-frame, near the notice that said Frank Bockwith could sell beer and spirits, and that singing was permitted on the premises.

Nobody came for a long time, and Porky was just about to give the bell another impatient jab, when the narrow double door opened. It was Maria Barbara. I heaved a sigh of relief. She looked at me and grinned, but looked at the boys, very puzzled.

'Maria Barbara. This is my brother Teddy and Porky Johnson. We all want to see your granda. It's very important.'

'Alright then,' she agreed, but her face was still puzzled as she led the way through the bar through to the back room. In there, the fire was blazing as though it had never been out since yesterday. I noticed Maria Barbara had a sort of dressing gown on, all swirly multi-coloured silk, with a wide sash at the waist. She reminded me of that lady on Mam's precious Willow Pattern jug. We all stood about, and I felt very hot.

Maria Barbara coughed. 'I'll just go and get him then. He's still in bed, and he might be a bit cross at being got up,' and with a rustle of silk she vanished. We stood about, looking at the ornaments on the mantlepiece, and the pictures with the big heavy frames on the walls. We daren't sit down, but we felt out of place standing up, sort of making the place untidy.

'What's all this then, gettin' a man up from his hard-earned rest. Do you realise I was working till one o'clock this morning?' He sounded very cross, and seemed to bulge in all directions out of his checked, woolly dressing gown. He had no beret on and his hair was all thin and wispy and sticking out in all directions.

'We are sorry,' I mumbled and to my horror I felt my eyes filling with thick wet tears, and my nose itched like mad. He must have noticed this because his look and his tone softened.

'Anyway what are you all standing around like blinking candles for? Sit yourselves down, so I can have a good look at you. We all sat, and he peered at Teddy. 'Well I never, Charlie Wintersgill to the life. You've got to be Charlie's boy. Right down to the guilty look he always had when he'd been up to summat.' He looked across at Porky. 'Who are you then?'

'Called Porky—Peter Johnson.'

'Can't place you, but I bet I've served your Pa a pint or two in my time. Summat familiar about you too.'

When I knew Mr. Bockwith better, I came to recognise this habit he had of identifying all the faces he met, and his pride in his knowledge of family histories.

He looked from one to the other, and his face became sharp again. 'Well! Come on. Tell a man what dragged him out of bed, will you?'

We all started to gabble at once, and he roared at me, 'You tell!'

I told him how it all started. He raised his eyebrows at the theft of the books, and stopped me when I got to the treasure box.

'Gold coins? There was a tale in the family of me Da collecting coins, but nobody ever found any.'

I went on to tell how the box had forced us to return all our other booty in the middle of the night, and how we had watched the thieves at work. He cocked his round head on one side as I told how we had followed them through the dark streets just to find where they lived.

'But we didn't dare tell anybody what we knew cause of the things we took in the first place. It was only cause I met Maria Barbara by accident, and came here by accident, that we dared to come here today.'

'Thought I was a soft old touch who wouldn't do nought about it?'

'Granda!' Maria Barbara's voice was sharp and I could feel my eyes filling up again.

'Hey, sorry lass, I didn't mean to carp. Must a taken a gut or two to come even now. The thing is, what to do about getting my stuff back.'

Teddy spoke for the first time. 'We thought you might tell the cops you had had a 'nonymous phone call, and they could get it back without us being involved at all.'

'Fair idea. But what am I going to do about the coins? I didn't put them on the list of items missing that I gave to the police, so they'll be very suspicious if I suddenly claim such valuable things.'

We were all quiet, thinking so hard that you could nearly see the thoughts ballooning out of our heads like you see in those comics. Then Porky spoke up.

'You might not like the idea, mister, but its the only way to get back the treasure box without the police asking any questions. We'll go and get it for you, off them, just like we got it off you in the first place.'

'You mean pinch it off them,' Mr. Bockwith sounded very doubtful, and I thought of that cruel head covered by a stocking and shuddered.

'It's the only way. Then you can get the police to go as though you just had a tip-off, and they can get your other things back.'

'I promise, I wouldn't have you young'ns involved anyway, but I'm not sure of this, not sure at all. I'd rather get nothing back at all than . . .'

'What about giving us till dinner time to try and get it?' said Teddy. 'Then get the cops in to go and get the other stuff.'

Mr. Bockwith looked from one to the other. With his hair sticking up all over like that, he had a bit of a mad look. His eyes were a whitish grey and even at this time of the day looked bright and alive. His eyes kept coming back to Teddy.

'Hey, lad, tha't thee father's double. It could just be him standin' there starin' at us. Ginger top and all.' He grinned suddenly, showing many gaps in strangely white teeth. 'Alright then, give it a go. And if ye get knocked in the meanwhile, it'll learn you not to put your nose in. I'll give you till twelve o'clock.'

'Thanks,' said Teddy, and really it was as though there were only him and Mr. Bockwith in the room. It was another half an hour before we got away, as Mr. Bockwith started to ask us about our Dad, and how Mam was managing. Teddy even told the old man about Mam probably getting laid off, which I thought was a bit much. We really hardly knew the man. Then we all had cocoa and toast off a tray, which was what Mr. Bockwith and Maria Barbara had every day, apparently. Then we left, eager to get on with the job of getting back the treasure box.

We had just got out of the door of 'The Grapes', when a shout stopped us. We looked up. Maria Barbara was at a top window. 'Please wait a few moments. I'm coming.'

The boys looked at each other and groaned, but I was thrilled. It would be good to have someone of my own along, instead of tagging on behind the boys. They were already starting to dawdle on, but I stood tight waiting for Maria Barbara. She was out in a minute, dressed in a jumper and jeans, just like me. We raced along to catch up with the boys. When we reached them they took no notice of us whatsoever, so we went on ahead and pretended we weren't with them.

It took us nearly twenty minutes to make our way across the town to Baker Street. In broad daylight, it was a different journey again to the frightening night journey. There were women with prams, and children dragging on the handles, there were men on the corners standing gossiping. Cars and vans whizzed past, and the whitish autumn sunshine showed up leaning walls and the sunken rooves in this older part of the town.

'This is it.' Porky shouted to us. We ran back and peered up at the sign. It was muddy and hard to read even in daylight, but it did say Bakery Street.

'You said Baker Street,' objected Maria Barbara.

'Well it was one o'clock in the morning. What do you expect,' retorted Porky, rather rudely I thought.

'Don't squabble,' ordered Teddy. 'What about our plan of action. We can't just go up and knock on the door and ask for our treasure box back, can we?'

'Mmm' said Porky. 'Have to keep watch and make sure they come out, then we can look the place over.'

'If we just hang around, somebody's sure to notice and think we're up to no good,' I said.

'Which we are,' put in Maria Barbara, and we

all laughed and screamed as though this were very funny.

'I know,' said Teddy at last, wiping his eyes, 'you girls play hopscotch out the front of the house, and we'll play kicky out the back with Porky's ball.' Porky always had a ball in his pocket, and on this morning he also had a stub of chalk, so we could set up our hopscotch properly.

We walked along, and Teddy drew us a hopscotch directly outside Number 5. The men would have to walk over us to get out, so we wouldn't really miss them. We set about playing our game, without really concentrating on it, and the boys vanished round the back. I had to show Maria Barbara how to play, as she'd never played it before. She'd never even played in a street before. I felt very sorry for her.

Half an hour later, I was bending down marking out the four again because we had stubbed it out with our feet, when the door opened and two men came out. I crouched down as they passed and they took no more notice of me than if I were the pavement. I saw the bushy sticking up hair and I knew that they were the same men. We waited for them to get to the end of the street, and raced round the back to tell the boys.

'Sure they were the same?' asked Teddy.

'Positive.'

'Good. You go back round the front and keep Cavey. If they come back run round and give us a shout.'

We didn't like being away from the action, but somebody had to watch for the men. We had just started our game again, when Teddy came racing round. 'You'll have to go, May. There's only a pantry window open, and there's only you can get in, you're the smallest.'

We left Maria Barbara on guard and raced round the back again. Porky was ready with a beer crate underneath a small pantry window on the end of a gable. It was pushed right open and I reckoned I could squeeze in. I stood up on the crate. 'There's all plates and things here.'

'Move them, idiot!'

I moved a few piles away from the window on to another shelf and I got my head and shoulders into the window-space. The boys pushed and pushed me through, holding on to my feet so that I didn't fall inside, just sort of walked in on my hands. I crashed a few plates on to the floor, but finally stood up in the narrow space. The pantry door pushed open easy and I was into the kitchen.

I looked round. Where should I start looking? Where would they have hidden the treasure box? The kitchen was small and square, dominated by a big range that wasn't black and sparkling like Mr. Bockwith's, but grey looking and dingy, and the only sign of a fire was a faint curl of smoke from the ashy mess in the grate. There was a square table in the middle of the room covered with newspaper, and two easy chairs beside the fire.

Against the back wall was a big dresser with glass fronts, the kind they called a press. The shelves were littered with all sorts of rubbish like string and papers, tin cans and jugs. There was a pretty sort of fretwork top to it, all curly and patterny. I looked at it in admiration. Some piece of furniture, that. I was just about to look away when my eye was caught by something behind the fretwork. A square black shape. The Treasure box!

I pulled a high-backed chair over from the table, and clambered up on to the middle flat part of the press. I could just reach the box, and it took a few minutes to get my fingers under it to lift it out. I dropped it on to the shelf on which I was standing and jumped down. I couldn't resist opening the box to see if the coins were still there. Yes. There were the velvet cases, and the washleather bags. I could feel myself smiling with pleasure.

There was a piercing whistle from out the back, Cave! The men were coming. I dashed through to the kitchen with the box, unbolted the door, and rushed out. The boys were still beside the small window, looking anxious.

'Here I am. Didn't think I'd climb out through that hole did you?' I gave Teddy the box, and he didn't say a word, just grabbed my arm and rushed me through the back gate.

We ran along the back and met Maria who was running to meet us. 'They've gone in now,' she

said, 'but there's a police car coming down the street.' Porky peered round the corner. 'It's stoping at number 5. Bockwith must have tipped them off. Good job you got out in time, May, or the cops would have nabbed you!'

I groaned and said, 'Let's get back.' We walked back to the Grapes in a cluster, all of us looking again and again at the box that meant so much to us. We felt as if it were ours, but we knew it wasn't. I was quite happy to take it back to Mr. Bockwith away from those horrible men who had really stolen it, not just borrowed it like we did.

*   *   *

Back at the Grapes, Mr. Bockwith had got dressed, and had his black beret on. He stood up and welcomed us, with open arms. 'Thank goodness you're alright. It got round to twelve and you weren't back and I thought those villains had got you or summat. So I rang the police and told them I'd had an anonymous tip that that was about where those men lived that did the pub.'

'May just got out in time.' Maria Barbara said with a pride that made me pretty warm. 'She was the only one small enough to climb in.'

'Barbara! You went too! What on earth——'

Teddy interrupted him. 'Anyway, here's the box.' He put it on the table. The old man opened it up and exclaimed, as he turned over all the treasures inside. 'Fancy this being out our back, and I never knew. I never knew. A good job you found it, or it'd probably have gone for the ragman. Very valuable it must be, me granda's old collection.'

The telephone rang out in the bar and he went out, Maria Barbara and I set all the velvet lined boxes out on the table, and opened them, and got the coins out of their washleather bags, and placed them on the bags in rows. As we were doing this we gave the dull ones a bit of a polish. The old man was out in the bar a good time, as there were customers as well as the telephone in the bar.

When he came back, he said. 'That was the police.' The police had told him they had arrested the men, as they had found the money in a drawer, and the men had confessed. The men had apparently been quite shaken by another matter. The sergeant had thought they were quite potty, rambling on about gold coins, but Mr. Bockwith hadn't reported any gold coins missing, and there were certainly none at the house. Mr. Bockwith laughed at this and we all joined in. His eyes dropped to the splendid array on the table.

'By, that's a sight,' he said, and turned his eye on all of us. 'Now what shall we do about you lot?' I knew he wasn't going to tell us off, because of the twinkle in his light eyes. 'How about you having a coin each? Then you'd always remember this little adventure, and it might remind you that taking things isn't really worth the trouble, even if you don't call it stealing.'

We all crowded round and chose one. Maria Barbara too, as she was involved in the end of the adventure.

*   *   *

'And that,' concluded Auntie May, 'was how I got that coin, that our Robert is clutching in his sweaty little palm at this very moment.'

Robert opened his hand to look at the gold coin that lay glittering there. Auntie May gave him a quick hug, and stood up, which made him stand up as well. He looked at her, and could easily see the little girl struggling to please her big brother —probably a girl like Pearl, who was standing up now and rubbing her eyes.

'What happened next?' demanded Gabbi.

'Next? Oh, well, lots of things, I suppose. We had lots of good times together, and Maria Barbara has always been my good friend. Is even now.'

'Auntie Ba,' shouted the two eldest girls together.

'That's right. We had many adventures as we grew up but that one was the most important, because that's when we made friends. Oh, and Granpa Bockwith ended up giving Mam a job at the Grapes, with good pay. So in the end she could meet me from school, although she still worked dinnertime and evenings.'

'And Teddy?' asked Robert, knowing the answer

before it came.

Auntie May looked at him with her very bright eyes, and laughed. ' "Hey lad," as Grandpa Bockwith used to say, "you're the spitting image of your Da." '

They were still laughing at this when uncle Peter came in. Robert knew him, as he had met Robert and his mother at the station when they had first arrived, and had driven them from Durham. Robert liked him, just looking at him. He was very big and muscular to look at, and mother had said that he had been County Tennis champion when he was younger. He taught Biology at Caldwell Road Grammar, but you would never have known him as a teacher, somehow.

'Somebody's having a good time, then!'

'Yeah, we've had a great time, Dad,' said Pearl. 'Mammy's been telling us all about when she was young, and about Teddy who was really Robert's Dad, and a gold coin . . .'

'Hold your noise, a minute, Pearl,' ordered Auntie May. 'It's past time for Robert to be home, and Daddy can drive him back before he gets his coat off. I'll have dinner ready when you get back, Peter.' They smiled at each other and May was bustling the man and the boy out within a minute.

Robert enjoyed going home with Uncle Peter, with the big car eating up the blackness of the road, and the lights of other cars building up and then vanishing as they passed.

'So you heard the story of the gold coin?'

'Yes. I never realised those things really happened.'

'It's surprising. We had some good times in those days.'

'You as well?'

'Oh. Didn't you realise?' I have a coin too . . .'

'But you can't be Porky! He was fat and——'

'Yes, it did take me a few years to persuade your Auntie May I wasn't as bad as she thought I was.'

Robert looked up at Peter and thought how much people could change, or else how one person's idea of another could be wrong. Porky had never been quite as bad as May had thought . . .

'Here we are, anyway. I'll not come in. Nice to have another man in the family though. Sometimes feel crowded in with women.'

'I bet,' said Robert feelingly.

'Anyway, I'll call one day after school, and perhaps we could fix up about some fishing. What about that?'

'Great,' said Robert, getting out of the car, 'see you then.'

With a cheery wave, and a roar of his engine, Uncle Peter was away.

Robert rang the bell and his mother answered immediately. Her anxious face broke into a smile when she saw him. 'You're so late. I thought you must have lost yourself somehow.'

'I was alright. Uncle Peter brought me home.'

'Did you enjoy yourself?'

'Yes. It was good. All girls though. Uncle Peter said he would take me fishing, and Auntie May told me all about Dad when he was little.'

'That's nice. Perhaps you'll like being here after all.'

'I was bound to like it really, in the end, wasn't I? Seeing as I belong here, like Daddy?'

IF YOU HAVE ENJOYED THIS BOOK YOU MAY ALSO LIKE THESE:

THE BLACK PEARL *by Scott O'Dell*   20p

552 52008 X   Carousel Fiction

The Black Pearl belonged to the old men, with legends and stories to tell to pass the time—or so Ramon Salazar had thought, until he came face to face with the devilfish and the struggle for the pearl began. But Ramon had more than the dangers of the sea to conquer. Others wanted the Great Pearl of Heaven, including the evil Pearler from Seville.

TO VANISHING POINT *by Doreen Norman*   20p

552 52003 9   Carousel Fiction

There was a strange glow in the playground. Leaves were blowing round on the ground, but in a perfect circle. Then Hazel noticed something else, something which, somehow, no-one but herself could see. A girl was standing looking at her, a silver girl, from another planet.

OPERATION SIPPACIK *by Rumer Godden*   20p

552 52009 8   Carousel Fiction

It took a war to prove the heroism of Sippacik, when she was sent out on a vital mission for the 27th Battery, Royal Artillery, stationed in Cyprus. 'Seytan'—devil—was the name Arif Ali had given her, but to her owner Sippacik was the cleverest donkey in Cyprus. She had to be, she was about to face the enemy. This is her true story.

DUNN ON THE OCEAN FLOOR

y Williams and Raymond Abrashkin 25p

552 52012 8   Carousel Fiction

In his next adventure, Danny Dunn and his friends Irene
and Joe accompanied Professor Bullfinch and Dr. Grimes to
the seabed in their Bathyscaphe on a scientific quest. Danny
took along his tape recorder to record the noises made by
the fishes—and that's what started the trouble!

ARCHIE—YOUNG DETECTIVE *by Robert Bateman* 25p

552 52006 3   Carousel Fiction

Something suddenly moves in the club-house, a shadow that
shouldn't be there. Archie stops to listen. He doesn't look
much like a detective, but when his best friend is accused of
stealing money from the club Henry Archibald McGilli-
cuddy gets his chance to play at being policeman.